CARL'S HALLOWEEN

ALEXANDRA DAY

MARGARET FERGUSON BOOKS
Farrar Straus Giroux
New York

Thank you to Penelope Alar Darling, Archimedes and Declan Darling, and all the Denny Blaine children who posed for me in their fine costumes. —A.D.

Farrar Straus Giroux Books for Young Readers
120 Broadway, New York, NY 10271

Copyright © 2015 by Alexandra Day
Printed in China by RR Donnelley Asia Printing Solutions Ltd.,
Dongguan City, Guangdong Province
Designed by Roberta Pressel
First edition, 2015
10   9   8   7   6   5   4   3

mackids.com

Library of Congress Cataloging-in-Publication Data
Day, Alexandra, author, illustrator.
    Carl's Halloween / Alexandra Day. — First edition.
        pages cm.
    Summary: "Carl and Madeleine dress up in costume and go out on a
Halloween adventure"— Provided by publisher.
    ISBN 978-0-374-31082-0 (hardback)
[1. Halloween—Fiction.   2. Rottweiler dog—Fiction.   3. Dogs—Fiction.]
I. Title.

PZ7.D32915Caru 2015
[E]—dc23
                                                2014041383

Farrar Straus Giroux Books for Young Readers may be purchased for business or promotional use.
For information on bulk purchases please contact Macmillan Corporate and Premium Sales Department
at (800) 221-7945 x5442 or by email at specialmarkets@macmillan.com.

The Carl character originally appeared in *Good Dog, Carl* by Alexandra Day, published by Green Tiger Press

"Trick or treat!"

"I have to go help Grandma for a little while. You can hand out candy to any children who come."

"I am so sorry,
but I wasn't
able to get any
candy this
year."

"Thank you, Carl. Now I will be able to make the trick-or-treaters happy!"

PLUNK
THE
PUMPKIN

10
20
30
50
75
100

MUMMY-WRAP GAME ←